Mrs. Noodlekugel and Four Blind Mice

The Zany Adventures of Mrs. Noodlekugel

Mrs. Noodlekugel

Mrs. Noodlekugel and Four Blind Mice

Mrs. Noodlekugel and Drooly the Bear

Mrs. Noodlekugel
AND Four Blind Mice

Daniel Pinkwater

illustrated by
Adam Stower

CANDLEWICK PRESS

Text copyright © 2013 by Daniel Pinkwater
Illustrations copyright © 2013 by Adam Stower

First paperback edition 2015

Library of Congress Catalog Card Number 2012947756
ISBN 978-0-7636-5054-4 (hardcover)
ISBN 978-0-7636-7658-2 (paperback)

14 15 16 17 18 19 BVG 10 9 8 7 6 5 4 3 2 1

Printed in Berryville, VA, U.S.A.

This book was typeset in Esprit.
The illustrations were done in ink.

Candlewick Press
99 Dover Street
Somerville, Massachusetts 02144

visit us at www.candlewick.com

To Jill, of course
D. P.

For Terry, Zita, and Harvey
A. S.

Chapter 1

Mrs. Noodlekugel's little house was in a sort of backyard behind a tall apartment building. The house was built long before the apartment buildings that had grown up all around it. Mrs. Noodlekugel lived with her cat, Mr. Fuzzface, and four fat mice. Nick and Maxine, a human boy and girl, brother and sister, lived in one of the apartment buildings. They discovered the hidden backyard and the little house, and Mrs. Noodlekugel, and became friends.

Mrs. Noodlekugel also became the children's babysitter. They would visit her in the little house when their parents were away, and sometimes when they were not. Very often, they would have tea and cookies with Mrs. Noodlekugel, Mr. Fuzzface, and the mice.

One day, the mice were making a terrible mess, spreading cookie crumbs everywhere, and spilling tea.

"The mice are becoming very far-sighted," Mrs. Noodlekugel said. "It is not that they have bad table manners, just that they do not see very well. There is nothing to do but take them downtown and have them fitted with eyeglasses."

"I was thinking the same," said Mr. Fuzzface, Mrs. Noodlekugel's cat.

"We will take them tomorrow," Mrs. Noodlekugel said. "Children, would you like to come along? We will go on the bus. You can help us, and it will be interesting."

"You want us to come with you on the bus?" Nick and Maxine asked.

"If you don't mind," Mrs. Noodlekugel said. "Mr. Fuzzface has to go in
a cat carrier—it is a rule of the bus

company. I have such a cat carrier. I will ask Mike the janitor to get it from the attic. Then you children could help me carry him."

Mike the janitor mopped the floors and carried out the garbage and fixed things around the apartment building. Sometimes he also helped Mrs. Noodlekugel. Nick and Maxine knew him. He had a blue chin and a mustache like a brush, and liked to sit in a little room in the basement, eating stewed tomatoes out of a can, talking to himself and listening to the radio.

"We will have to ask our parents," Nick and Maxine said.

"I am sure they will agree," Mrs. Noodlekugel said. "It is a perfectly respectable bus company."

Chapter 2

Nick and Maxine turned up at Mrs. Noodlekugel's house in the morning with a note from their parents saying they could go. Mrs. Noodlekugel had on her coat and a hat with flowers and plastic cherries. She was trying to coax Mr. Fuzzface into a cat carrier, which

was like a big handbag with a little screened window.

"It is wrong to make me ride in that thing," Mr. Fuzzface said.

"It is only for a little while," Mrs. Noodlekugel said. "And it is a rule of the bus company."

"I object to being treated like an animal," Mr. Fuzzface said.

"I understand," Mrs. Noodlekugel said.

"It is undignified," Mr. Fuzzface said.

"It is," Mrs. Noodlekugel said.

"I protest," Mr. Fuzzface said.

"But you want to come along," Mrs. Noodlekugel said. "You want to come downtown with the children and the mice and me, do you not?"

"Yes."

"And you want to visit the oculist, so the mice can be fitted with eyeglasses, and afterward we will go and have something nice to eat. You would like that, wouldn't you?"

"May I order anything I want?" Mr. Fuzzface asked.

"Of course," Mrs. Noodlekugel said.

"Ice cream and sardines?" Mr. Fuzz-face asked.

"If you want," Mrs. Noodlekugel said.

"I will ride in the cat carrier," Mr. Fuzzface said. "But it is wrong."

"It is this way every time we go anywhere," Mrs. Noodlekugel said to Nick and Maxine.

"But where are the mice?" Nick asked.

"Oh, I did not forget the mice," Mrs. Noodlekugel said. "Look closely at my hat."

Nick and Maxine looked closely at Mrs. Noodlekugel's hat. Among the plastic cherries and flowers, the four mice were attached to the hat by elastic bands around their middles.

"They are quite safe and secure," Mrs. Noodlekugel said.

"The mice get to look out the windows of the bus," Mr. Fuzzface said from inside the cat carrier. "They do not have to ride in a stuffy cat carrier. Why can't I ride on your hat?"

"You are too big to ride on my hat," Mrs. Noodlekugel said. "Now let us go and wait for the bus."

Chapter 3

Mrs. Noodlekugel and the children waited for the bus. When the bus came, she said to the driver, "One grown-up, two children, and a cat."

"Full fare for the adult, half fare for the children, fifteen cents for the cat," the driver said.

"There are mice on my hat," Mrs. Noodlekugel said.

"No charge for mice on hats," the driver said. "Do not let them run loose."

"Of course not," Mrs. Noodlekugel said. "Come, children, let's move back in the bus and take seats."

Nick and Maxine took a seat with Mr. Fuzzface in the cat carrier between them.

Mrs. Noodlekugel sat in the seat behind them. The mice looked out the bus window, and Mr. Fuzzface told a story.

"I was a railroad cat. I would ride
with the engineer. At night I would
sit on the engineer's shoulder and
look ahead for obstacles on the tracks,
because cats, as you know, have
excellent night vision. During the day
I would sleep in the engineer's hat.

The railroad men fed me ham sand-
wiches and pickles. I was famous up
and down the railroad.

"I was the one who prevented a
train wreck on the Poughkeepsie railroad bridge. The signal had gone out,
and I sat on the track blinking one
eye, and then the other.
Cats' eyes shine in the
dark, as you know,
and when my eyes
were picked up
in the headlights
of the oncoming
train, the brave

22

engineer brought it to a stop and saved many lives. The president of the railroad gave me a gold medal, which, as you can see, I wear on my collar to this day. Mrs. Noodlekugel has one just like it."

"Mrs. Noodlekugel does?"

"Yes, Mrs. Noodlekugel was the engineer driving that train. It was how we met."

Nick asked, "Mrs. Noodlekugel, you were a railroad engineer?"

"Oh, yes, I was the only lady engineer for many years. And Mr. Fuzzface was a famous railroad cat."

"My father, Oldface, was a railroad cat, too," Mr. Fuzzface said. "He was the engineer's cat on Old 97, on the Lynchburg-to-Danville run. I don't remember him very well, but my mother, Momface, told me stories about him. One night he disappeared. We looked for him everywhere. I still look for him — a long and skinny yellow cat with one ragged ear and a squinty eye. It is my greatest wish to find my long-lost daddy."

"You want to find him because you miss him so much," Maxine said.

"He left my mother to raise seven kittens all by herself," Mr. Fuzzface said. "I want to bite him. If I ever run into him, I will teach him a lesson."

"Now, Mr. Fuzzface," Mrs. Noodle-kugel said, "perhaps Oldface had a reason for disappearing. You know, it's a mighty hard road from Lynchburg to Danville, and you have to make a three-mile grade."

"I will give him ten seconds to explain," Mr. Fuzzface said. "After that I will be all over him like sardines on ice cream."

"Look! There is the oculist's!" Mrs. Noodlekugel said. "Let us go in."

The oculist's shop was full of shiny glass cases. In the cases were pairs of shiny eyeglasses. There were strange-looking machines and a special chair to sit in while being examined.

Chapter 4

"Let us get off the bus," Mrs. Noodle-kugel said. "We are downtown, and we have arrived."

Mrs. Noodlekugel, with the four mice on her hat, and Nick and Maxine, carrying Mr. Fuzzface in the cat carrier, got off the bus.

"Hello, Mrs. Noodlekugel," Dr. Bril, the oculist, said. "Hello, children. And I see you have brought Mr. Fuzzface. Hello, cat. What may I do for you all today?"

"These mice on my hat need their eyes examined," Mrs. Noodlekugel said.

"Ah, mice," Dr. Bril said. "I will need to stack some books on the seat of my special examination chair so they will be high enough."

Dr. Bril carried thick books and stacked them on the seat of the special examination chair. Mrs. Noodlekugel helped the mice get out of the elastic bands that held them to her hat and helped the first mouse get to the top of the stack of books.

"The mice cannot read, of course," Dr. Bril said.

"No, they are mice," Mrs. Noodle-kugel said.

"Ordinarily, we test vision with an eye chart," Dr. Bril said. "It has large letters at the top, smaller letters underneath, and still smaller letters underneath those, and so on until the letters are very small. But that would not do with these mice."

"No, it would not," Mrs. Noodle-kugel said.

"So, I will use this special eye chart, made for mice," Dr. Bril said. "As you see, there is a picture of a mouse in a cowboy hat, a cat, and a piece of cheese at the top, quite large. Beneath that is a picture of a piece of cheese, a cat, and a mouse in a cowboy hat, somewhat smaller. The next line has a picture of a cat, a mouse in a cowboy hat, and a piece of cheese, smaller yet, and so on. I will point to each picture, and the mouse will tell me what it sees."

"The mice cannot talk, either," Mrs. Noodlekugel said.

"Well, we will do our best," Dr. Bril said. He pointed to the largest picture of a mouse in a cowboy hat. The mouse on top of the stack of books clapped its paws and jumped up and down.

Then Dr. Bril pointed to the largest picture of a cat. The mouse stroked its whiskers.

He pointed to the largest picture of a piece of cheese, and the mouse rubbed its belly.

"This is satisfactory," Dr. Bril said. "We will continue." He pointed to the pictures on the next line, and the line after that. The mouse clapped its paws, stroked its whiskers, and rubbed its belly.

This continued, until when Dr. Bril pointed to a picture, the mouse became confused and scratched its head. Then Dr. Bril made a note on a little card.

"This mouse has musopia," Dr. Bril said. "We can fit eyeglasses for that. Now let us test the next mouse."

When he had tested all the mice, Dr. Bril said, "I will go into the back room and make the eyeglasses. Please wait here. You may read magazines and look at the pictures on the walls."

Chapter 5

After a little while, Dr. Bril came out of the back room with four tiny pairs of eyeglasses. "I have chosen frames in red, yellow, blue, and green so the mice will not get their eyeglasses mixed up." He carefully put a pair of eyeglasses on each mouse.

The mice peered through their new eyeglasses. They looked at each other, and at the pictures on the walls. They looked all around the oculist's shop. They turned this way and that, faster and faster. They squeaked excitedly.

They then began to scurry. They scurried all around the shop. They climbed the shelves, got on top of tables and chairs, peered out the shop window, spun until they were dizzy, and danced in a circle.

"The mice appear to be happy with their new eyeglasses," Mrs. Noodlekugel said.

"Yes, they are seeing much better," Dr. Bril said. "They are enjoying it."

Mrs. Noodlekugel thanked Dr. Bril. Dr. Bril said good-bye to the mice, gave lollipops in the shape of eyeglasses to Nick and Maxine, and patted Mr. Fuzzface on the head.

Chapter 6

The mice struggled and kicked and refused to ride attached to Mrs. Noodlekugel's hat with elastic bands. They wanted to walk on the sidewalk. So did Mr. Fuzzface.

"You must hold paws and stay together," Mrs. Noodlekugel told the mice. "And on the bus going home, you must ride on my hat."

Nick and Maxine heard a tiny gurgling noise. "What is that?" they asked.

"It is the mice," Mrs. Noodlekugel said. "Their tummies are rumbling. They are hungry."

"So am I," Mr. Fuzzface said. "Are we going to a restaurant?"

"Yes. We will walk along until we find one," Mrs. Noodlekugel said.

So they walked along, Mrs. Noodlekugel leading the way, Nick and Maxine carrying Mr. Fuzzface's empty cat carrier, the mice holding paws and looking all around through their new eyeglasses, with Mr. Fuzzface following behind, making sure the mice got into no trouble.

"Stay together," Mrs. Noodlekugel said. "We are looking for a nice restaurant."

They came to a place with a sign over the door: DIRTY SALLY'S LUNCHROOM.

"Here is a nice place," Mrs. Noodle-kugel said.

"Dirty Sally's Lunchroom?" Nick asked.

"It doesn't have a very nice name," Maxine said.

"I am sure it is nice," Mrs. Noodlekugel said. "Only a good restaurant would have a disgusting name like that. They must call it that to discourage the timid. We can go in."

Chapter 7

In Dirty Sally's Lunchroom, none of the chairs matched, and the tables wobbled. The walls were painted pea green, and the floor was covered with yellow linoleum that was old and scuffed. There was a counter at one side of the room where some old men were eating Nesselrode pie.

"Oh, it is charming!" Mrs. Noodlekugel said. "Let us sit at a table and
decide what we want to order."

They sat at a table, which wobbled.

"Look!" Maxine whispered. "The waiter is a monkey!"

Mrs. Noodlekugel turned and looked. "So he is. He is quite tall for a monkey."

The monkey waiter came to the table carrying a tray with glasses of water. He put a glass of water before Mrs. Noodlekugel, Maxine, and Nick and a saucer of water in front of Mr. Fuzzface. He saw the mice and brought tiny cups of water for them. Then he put a card on the table. Printed on the card was, *Tell the monkey what you want.*

"I suppose the monkey cannot speak," Mrs. Noodlekugel said.

"I would like ice cream with sardines on top," Mr. Fuzzface said.

The monkey held up a card that read, *We don't have that.*

"Do you have ice cream?" Mrs. Noodlekugel asked.

The monkey held up a card that read, *YES.*

"Do you have sardines?"

The monkey held up a card that read, *NO*.

"Mr. Fuzzface, they have ice cream, but they do not have sardines," Mrs. Noodlekugel said. "Would you like ice cream without sardines?"

"Absolutely not," Mr. Fuzzface said. "There is no point in eating ice cream without sardines."

"Perhaps you will allow me to order for us all," Mrs. Noodlekugel said. To the waiter she said, "Do you have cheesecake?"

The monkey held up a card that read:

Try Dirty Sally's
FAMOUS
CHEESECAKE

"We will have four pieces of cheese-cake," Mrs. Noodlekugel said. "And one piece of cheesecake cut into four for the mice. And tea. We will have tea."

The monkey nodded and went away.

"Cheesecake? What is cheesecake?" Maxine and Nick asked. "It sounds awful. Does it have Swiss cheese? Does it have cheddar cheese?"

"It is made with cream cheese," Mrs. Noodlekugel said. "It is very nice, and you will like it."

The monkey waiter brought four big pieces of cheesecake, one piece of cheesecake cut into four for the mice, a pot of tea, and cups. Even cut into four, the pieces of cheesecake were as big as the mice. The mice sniffed, tasted, and rubbed their bellies. Nick and Maxine tasted their cheesecake.

"Yum," Nick said.

"Yum," Maxine said.

"This would be even better with sardines," Mr. Fuzzface said.

Chapter 8

Mrs. Noodlekugel poured tea and took dainty forkfuls of cheesecake. Nick and Maxine ate their cheesecake, *nom, nom, nom.* Mr. Fuzzface lapped his cheesecake. The mice nibbled for all they were worth.

"Yum!"

Nom!

Lap!

Nibble, nibble, nibble!

There was more cheesecake than any of them could finish. One by one, the children, Mr. Fuzzface, and Mrs. Noodlekugel sat back in their chairs to rest and wonder if they could eat another bite. The mice kept nibbling for all they were worth.

Then the mice began to switch their tails and bounce up and down. They pulled off chunks of cheesecake and threw them at one another. They squeaked and spun in circles, chasing their tails, and rolled on their backs, waving their tiny paws in the air.

"Mrs. Noodlekugel, the mice are behaving strangely," Maxine said.

"They are acting crazy," Nick said.

"They have eaten too much cheesecake," Mrs. Noodlekugel said. "It is going to their heads."

"It is the sugar," Mr. Fuzzface said. "They are not used to so much."

The mice climbed down the table leg and began to scurry all around Dirty Sally's Lunchroom. An old man came in to get some Nesselrode pie, and when he opened the door, the mice scurried out.

"Oh, my!" Mrs. Noodlekugel said. "The mice have gone outside! Come, children! Come, Mr. Fuzzface! We must go after them!" To the monkey waiter, she called, "We will come back! Do not take away our cheesecake!" And to the children and the cat, she called, "Let us hurry! We must collect the mice before they get into trouble!"

Chapter
9

Outside in the street, cars, trucks, and buses rumbled past. The sidewalk was crowded with people walking.

"Do you see the mice?" Mrs. Noodlekugel asked. "Look for the mice!"

The children and Mr. Fuzzface walked up and down, calling the mice.

"Here, mice!" they called. "Nice mousie, mousie, mousie! Where are you, mice?"

There was not a mouse to be seen.

A policeman came along. "We are looking for four runaway mice," Mrs. Noodlekugel told the policeman.

"Where did you see them last?" the policeman asked.

"Just here," Mrs. Noodlekugel said. "They ran out of the restaurant."

"Can you describe the mice?" the policeman asked.

"They are mice," Mrs. Noodlekugel said. "They are gray. They are small. There are four of them."

"What are their names?" the policeman asked.

"We just call them mice," Mrs. Noodlekugel said. "We do not know their names."

"I will help you look for them," the

policeman said. He began to walk up and down, looking for the mice. "Here, mice!" he called. "Nice mousie, mousie, mousie! Where are you, mice?"

There was not a mouse to be seen.

They came to a narrow space, an alley between two buildings.

"Let us look here," Mrs. Noodlekugel said.

In the alley, they saw four mice sitting on the lid of a garbage can. With them, on top of the garbage can, was a long and skinny yellow cat with one ragged ear and a squinty eye.

"Is dese your mices?" the cat said.

"Yes!" Mrs. Noodlekugel said. "Naughty mice! Why did you run away?"

The mice looked down at their feet and played with their whiskers nervously.

"Saw dese mices," the yellow cat said. "Mices not belong here. Told them sit still. Then think what do with mices. Then you come."

"So these are the mice?" the policeman asked.

"Yes, they are naughty mice," Mrs. Noodlekugel said.

"I am glad you found them," the policeman said. "I will be going now."

"Thank you for helping us look for the mice," Mrs. Noodlekugel said. "Will you join us for a cup of tea and a piece of cheesecake at Dirty Sally's?"

"Thank you," said the policeman. "May I have Nesselrode pie instead?"

"Of course," Mrs. Noodlekugel said. And to the yellow cat, she said, "We would like to thank you for taking care of the mice. Please join us, too."

"Want ice cream with sardines," the yellow cat said.

"They have no sardines," Mr. Fuzz-face said. "But the cheesecake is good."

"OK," said the yellow cat.

Chapter
10

Mrs. Noodlekugel, Nick and Maxine, Mr. Fuzzface, the four mice, the policeman, and the yellow cat were seated around the wobbly table.

"Please take the mice's cheesecake away," Mrs. Noodlekugel told the monkey waiter. "They have had enough. And please bring Nesselrode pie for the policeman and a piece of cheesecake for the yellow cat. They are our guests."

"Dis is nice," said the yellow cat.

"We were noticing that you can talk," Maxine said to the yellow cat.

"I noticed that, too," said the policeman.

"But you talk differently from me," Mr. Fuzzface said. "I was taught to speak by Mrs. Noodlekugel."

"Was learned to talk by rough sailor-men," the yellow cat said. "Probably why not talk nice like you."

"Are you an offshore kitty?" Mrs. Noodlekugel asked.

"First was railroad cat," the yellow cat said.

"I was a railroad cat," Mr. Fuzzface said. "And my father was a railroad cat."

"Took train to San Francisco," the yellow cat said. "In San Francisco, taken aboard big ship. Ship went away for years and years. Not able to write. Besides, didn't know anybody able to read. So can't send letter. Must have been like disappeared."

"My father disappeared," Mr. Fuzz-face said.

"Left seven kittens behind," the yellow cat said.

"I was one of seven kittens who were left behind," Mr. Fuzzface said.

"When finally came back, kittens gone, don't know where. Mate gone, don't know where."

"My mother went I don't know where," Mr. Fuzzface said.

"Mate was called Momface," the yellow cat said.

"My mother was called Momface," Mr. Fuzzface said.

The yellow cat looked at Mr. Fuzzface with his eye that was not squinty.
"What your name?"

"My name is Mr. Fuzzface," Mr.
Fuzzface said.

"Fuzzface, I yam yer fadder."

Chapter 11

Oldface?" Mr. Fuzzface asked.

"Oldface," the yellow cat said.

The two cats stared at each other across the table, Mr. Fuzzface with both eyes and Oldface with his good eye. No one said anything.

Nick and Maxine wondered if Mr. Fuzzface was going to bite his father, as he had said he would . . . but he didn't.

"I call this a remarkable coincidence," Mrs. Noodlekugel said.

"So do I," said the policeman, whose name was Officer Chestnut.

"And where do you live now, Mr. Oldface?" Mrs. Noodlekugel asked.

"Alley, where mices was, where you met," Oldface said.

"And is it satisfactory?" Mrs. Noodlekugel asked Oldface.

"Is alley," Oldface said. "Is wet when rains, is cold when snows."

"I was thinking, would you prefer to live in a little house, where it is dry when it rains and warm when it snows and there is plenty to eat?"

"You crazy, lady? Who wouldn't prefer?" Oldface said.

"Of course, there is the problem of the bus. We have only one cat carrier."

"I can arrange a ride in a police car," Officer Chestnut said.

"Oooh!" said Nick and Maxine.

"And of course, we have to ask Mr. Fuzzface," Mrs. Noodlekugel said. "Mr. Fuzzface, is it all right with you if Oldface comes and stays with us?"

"Of course it is all right," Mr. Fuzzface said. "He is my fadder."